It is with my deepest gratitude and warmest affection that I dedicate
This book to my sister
Stacie L. Potter
Who was a constant source of motivation and inspiration in my life.
May she rest in heaven.

The bright sun beams through the bedroom window as Claire rolls out of bed. It is Saturday which means no school and extra time for Claire to inspect her busy, wiggly tooth.

1

Claire takes a peek and notices that her tooth is even wigglier today than it was the day before.

Today, Claire is on a mission! She wiggles her busy tooth all day until suddenly it falls out.

"Mom," Claire yells. "My tooth! My tooth!"

4

Claire runs to her mom who is in the kitchen making dinner.

She wanted to show her mom her tooth before she put it underneath her pillow. Mom smiles and inspects Claire's fallen tooth.

"Mom, now that my tooth is out, how will the Tooth Fairy know to come to our house," Claire asked worriedly. "Does the Tooth Fairy have to travel to all the little boys and little girls that lose teeth or is there a special Tooth Fairy just for me?"

"Oh, Claire don't worry about that," Mom says.
"The Tooth Fairy knows exactly where to go."

"...but Mom," Claire continues. "Once the tooth is underneath my pillow, how will the Tooth Fairy know how to find it?"

"Claire, the Tooth Fairy just knows," Claire's mom insists. "Now let's get you ready for bed."

10

Claire desperately wanted answers to her questions, so she decides to stay awake to ask the Tooth Fairy herself.

11

Claire closes her eyes for what seems like a second and suddenly she sees the most beautiful sight. It's the Tooth Fairy and she looks more beautiful than Claire ever imagined!

12

Her dazzling dress swirled with purple and
white stripes while her sparkling pink and
purple heels shined so bright. Her purple polka
dot leggings matched her big curly hair and
with those pink whimsical wings,
Claire cannot help but stare.

13

The Tooth Fairy glides next to Claire's bed as if she is floating on air as **Claire notices the Tooth Fairy's large pockets stitched with shimmery thread.**

"Those must be there to hold all of the teeth," Claire whispered to herself.

The Tooth Fairy twirled her glowing, pink wand.
Claire just knows her wand is magic! It just must be!

15

"Miss Tooth Fairy," Claire nervously whispers.

The Tooth Fairy flashes her big, beautiful smile.
She reaches for Claire's hand and says, "Come with
me before we run out of time."

The Tooth Fairy gives Claire her very own magic wand and with just two shakes off they go into their night's journey! They visit what seems like a million houses, but the Tooth Fairy knows exactly where to go because her magical wand gleams every time they get close.

17

On the towering roof tops of India, they find
teeth nestled in colorful places.

18

Then they jet over to Spain rescuing teeth floating in pottery glasses.

19

At last, they scurry over to Africa finding
teeth hiding in fuzzy bath slippers.

Claire is so amazed at the wonderful places she gets to see, but the most amazing part is seeing what the Tooth Fairy would leave.

At each visit, the Tooth Fairy places each tooth carefully in her striped pockets, leaving each child a magical coin made just for them.

22

As they finish their route, Claire smiles at the thought of such a magical night. She did not want it to end but realizes that the last stop is the Tooth Fairy bringing Claire home.

They reach her house and the Tooth Fairy waves goodbye to Claire as she glides into the sky.

24

Suddenly Claire hears someone calling her name. "Claire rise and shine... it's time to get up," Mom shouts.

25

Claire jumps up with excitement! Claire thinks
it all must have been just a dream. Claire looks
under her pillow and sees the magical coin.

"Claire you left your play wand on the floor,"
Mom says reaching down to pick it up.

27

Claire's eyes grow big with amazement.

"It wasn't just a dream," Claire shouts. "I really did meet the Tooth Fairy!"

29

Mom grabs Claire's brown cheeks and says,
"Oh, Claire...how I just love your imagination."

CPSIA information can be obtained
at www.ICGtesting.com
Printed in the USA
LVHW020935020721
691696LV00002B/41

9 781737 468103